Reckoning

Stephen Baker

TSL Drama

Published in Great Britain in 2020
By TSL (Drama) Publications, Rickmansworth

Copyright © 2020 Stephen Baker

ISBN / 978-1-913294-58-8

Cover photo: https://pixabay.com/illustrations/hacker-computer-spirit-cyber-code-4031973/

Contents

Inbox

Mark is 38 and works as a housing officer for a local authority. The office where he works has undergone a substantial change. A new manager has come in and imposed new rules and regulations.

Setting:
Scene 1 & 2: Chair
Scene 2: Armchair

Performance time:
10 minutes

Scene One

Mark sits alone in the staff room at the housing office. He is smartly dressed.

Well, here it is, another day in paradise. I'm being sarcastic by the way. Before the new manager, Tony Newton, started I actually enjoyed my job. I may not have described the office as paradise, but it was pleasant, easy going. Everyone got on, no real animosity. That's how it was under the previous manager, Sharon. Then, she retired and was subsequently replaced by Newton who came straight from the army. Now the office is run like a military camp. We are told to be behind our desks ten minutes before the office opens at 9.00 a.m. At precisely 8.55 a.m. the door will burst open and in will stride Newton with a clipboard tucked under his arm. He does a general inspection of the troops, as he likes to call us, checking we are all smart and presentable. I got reported last week for not having a shave. He came right up to me he did, nose right in my face. 'And what do have here, then,' he said. I explained that I have sensitive skin and had developed a rash. 'Not good enough,' he said.

Pause

The incident was formally recorded in a staff log. I had to go to the office and be reprimanded, and was made to sign a form that he had completed, which was placed in my staff file. He warned me about future conduct. I've never been in trouble before. It was really upsetting. I have an exemplary work record. When Sharon was here she said she liked a relaxed office. She said it works better. Well someone ought to tell Newton. Some of us feel we've been enlisted. I have tried to talk to him about break times. He has regulated the time we can have a break to twelve minutes. As I tried to explain to him, our office is the furthest away from the staff room; so it takes us five minutes to get there. By the time we have boiled the kettle it's time to go back to our desks, or work stations as we are told they are now to be referred to. His response? 'Try drinking a cup of coffee when you are knee deep in mud in the freezing cold with bullets flying over your head.' All I wanted was for me and my colleagues to get a coffee break like everyone else.

Pause

And if the morning roll call isn't enough, you should see the staff meetings. They resemble something from a Nuremburg rally. His 'yes men' cheering and applauding at everything he says. Newton stands at the front and tells us we are going to be the best department in the council. I didn't realise it was a competition. I thought we were just here to help people. He reiterates that a disciplined team is an effective team. He has this message pinned on every staff notice board. It feels like a form of brain washing to me. He's also stopped any banter in the office. Nobody is allowed to talk to a work colleague unless it is work related. This guy is a complete control freak, and I'm really not sure how much more I can take.

Pause

My girlfriend Laura is a tutor at the local college. She teaches IT for beginners. And who is on her course? None other than Newton. The fact he is IT illiterate is a real concern, as it begs the question: how did he get the job, when more suitably qualified people are available within the department? I've heard he plays squash with the Director of Housing. Which might explain a lot. I'm sure when he learns the art of sending emails we will be bombarded with written instructions. At least we have some peace and quiet at the moment when we log into our computers. There's a feeling in the office that our computers are a safe place. I've a feeling all that is about to change.

Fade

Scene 2

Lights up

Mark sits in the staff room once again.

Newton has obviously been paying attention on his IT course. We are now told to check our inboxes on a daily basis as he has taken to emailing us instructions. I am getting rather tired of my inbox being clogged up with daily 'briefing notes' as he calls them. Then I got the shock of my life. I saw one of his emails marked: Private and Confidential. I opened it hesitantly. He was informing me that I was to be formally disciplined. The charge was not being suitably dressed for work. He elaborated by stating that I had been previously warned about such behaviour, which was the non-shaving incident. The new incident was that I had removed my tie without permission. It was sweltering hot. When Sharon was here she wasn't that concerned about what we wore. Smart but casual, was her view on work attire. As long as you didn't wear jeans and t-shirts it was fine. And nobody took advantage. We all came smartly dressed and practical depending on the weather. In winter we would wear a jumper, in summer the men would wear a short sleeved shirt, unbuttoned at the top. Then came the directive from Newton that men had to wear shirt and ties at all times, and the top button of the shirt must be fastened. On this particular day, Newton was out of the office and it was an exceptionally hot day, so I took my tie off and unbuttoned my top button. One of his 'yes men' will have reported me. Since Newton came, it feels as if you can't trust anyone.

Pause

Then worse was to come, at the end of the message it said that Newton had informed the union official, Davies, of my forthcoming hearing and that he was the allocated officer who would represent me. The problem is that it has been strongly rumoured that Davies is in his pocket. Newton has just promoted him. He represented one of the cleaners the other week on a disciplinary and never spoke up for her in the meeting. Newton reduced her to tears. Her crime? Not signing out some cleaning cloths from the stock room. She got a final written warning.

Pause

When I trailed through Newton's many emails, I came across the one marked 'disciplinary procedure changes'. He had amended the said procedures with Davies. When I read through the changes he had made, I realised I was up the Swannee without a paddle. Any member of staff on a disciplinary could only be represented by a union official who worked in the department. This meant I could not ask for anyone else except Davies. He had also changed the category of offence section. Now anyone receiving a formal reprimand, which I have, and who was then subsequently disciplined for a similar offence, would be charged with gross misconduct and could be dismissed.

Pause

I actually don't know what I am going to do. It's a nightmare. The email said I should wait further instructions of when my hearing will take place, and that I should contact Davies at the earliest opportunity to ensure that I am adequately represented. What a joke that is. I feel like the condemned man already.

Fade

Scene 3

Lights up

Mark sits in an armchair in a plush hotel lobby.

Just waiting for my better half, Laura to join me. We are having high tea in the dining hall of this lovely hotel. This is one of my little treats for her for standing by me over the last few months. I could never have coped without her.

Pause

I expect you're wondering what has happened since receiving my notice of a disciplinary hearing. Well, I can tell you an awful lot. When I first got the notification it seemed there was no light at the end of the tunnel. I was facing a disciplinary hearing with a 'lame duck' union official, and possible dismissal. It looked like I didn't have a leg to stand on.

Pause

I'm sure that Newton thought he had covered every angle with military precision. Well, unfortunately for him, not quite. He's now sitting at home minus his job and worried sick that I'll take his life savings off him. Which I am reliably informed I will. And what of Davies? You may ask. Sacked. Left in disgrace.

Pause

Let me tell you how everything unravelled. I contacted Davies as I was advised to do. The only thing he could advise was to check my inbox for further instruction. When Newton completed his IT course, he made the department use emails rather than paper, it costs less. So, every day I would check my inbox. Then, about a week after the original email in my inbox there was another email from Newton marked 'Disciplinary Notification.' I hesitantly opened it and read the first few lines. It read further to my last email, blah, blah, blah, and gave me the details of when and where the hearing was to held, who was representing me and that I was charged with gross misconduct. I was utterly devastated.

Pause

In fact I was so devastated that I broke down at my desk and had to be consoled by Carol who sits next to me. It was Carol who alerted me to something that was to turn everything on its head. She said, 'It's a bloody long email to tell you that you're being disciplined. You've barely scrolled down a couple of sentences. There's a load more in the email that you should read. It might be important.' And indeed it was. (*Smiles*). Newton in his ignorance had dropped the biggest clanger of his life. As I scrolled down the page I realised he had been liaising with Davies by email as regards my case. And without thinking he forwarded the whole lot with my email. He obviously was not as conversant with emails as he thought.

Pause

They had agreed that I would be dismissed. Apparently, Newton had been keeping a dossier on me. He had also been into my personnel file and disclosed some sensitive information. It was a clear breach of the data protection act. He also made some inappropriate comments about me. Carol advised I should see a solicitor. I contacted Laura, told her what happened and she spoke to a solicitor she knew. I was advised to resign on the grounds of constructive dismissal.

Pause

It went to a tribunal and I won a substantial amount. I am now suing Newton for libel, harassment and for using my data without my consent.

Pause

Funny how things work out sometimes. Ah, there's Laura. (*Gets up from the armchair.*) Well, must dash. Those sandwiches and cakes won't eat themselves.

Ends

Closure

David is in his early 50s. He hails from a small town in the North West of England, where he has always lived. He lives alone. He has been attending therapy sessions for depression and anxiety. He had an unhappy childhood.

Setting:

Scene 1 & 2: Chair

Scene 3: Park bench

Performance time:

10 minutes

Scene One

David sits in his lounge in his one bedroom flat.

Well that's another therapy session out of the way. I've been seeing a therapist for my depression and low self-esteem. My doctor referred me to a CPN. That's Community Psychiatric Nurse. Donna's her name. Nice girl. Not sure what she thinks of me. I'm a bit of a loner. Always have been, really. As a child I struggled to make friends. I just didn't know how to join in games and I was just a bit awkward really. I'm not sure how other children perceived me.

Pause

Anyway, I've been talking to Donna about my issues at school mainly. She feels that a lot of my problems come from experiences at school. She encourages me to talk about them and express myself. We don't just concentrate on the negative things, I'm encouraged to talk about the positive things as well, and let my feelings out. The negative experiences were the bullying that I endured at the hands of two boys who were in my year group when I got to secondary school, Stephen Baines and Brian Collins. Most of what we discuss ends up being about these two. The positive we discuss is generally about the love of my life. No, it's not a girl, or a boy for that matter! Before anyone gets the wrong idea. It's Manchester United. I just fell in love with the club from an early age. When I went to junior school everyone supported Liverpool. But I supported United. It wasn't a big deal. Nobody bothered me really. I was just kind of ignored. It might have been better for me if I had supported Liverpool. I could at least have had something to talk to the other kids about. But I was United, through and through.

Pause

I was born on 29th May 1968. The day United won the European Cup. The first English team to achieve this. My family supported United, and christened me David after one of the star players of that famous night – David Sadler. I could have been called George after George Best or Robert after Bobby Charlton, but my mother liked the name David, and the family felt that Sadler was an unsung hero from the final. My dad said he was United's best player on the night. Unfortunately, when I was at primary school in 1974 to be precise, they were

13

relegated from the First Division. And what made it worse, was that one of our idols for United, Denis Law, had signed for our biggest rivals – Manchester City. And at our own ground, Old Trafford, he only back heels the ball into our net and basically sent us down. I was there with my dad. He was close to tears. It was a terrible match really. Grown people crying. It was something a six year old shouldn't really experience.

Pause

I expect you're wondering if it was that which caused me to become depressed. Not really. We started winning again in the Second Division and came back up at the first time of asking. Everyone in the family was ecstatic. The only problem was that Liverpool had taken hold of the First Division in our absence and seemed unbeatable. Everyone, and I mean everyone, supported Liverpool. All the kids had Liverpool bags except me. I had a Man United bag. Liverpool was winning championships and the FA Cup, we got to the FA Cup final in 1976 but lost to Southampton, I got teased a bit about that. It was only banter. Nothing more. I could take it. Then the following year we were back at Wembley for another FA Cup final. And who were our opponents? Liverpool, no less. And we won 2-1. I really enjoyed going to school after that game. Even though we had won and I was the only United fan in the school, I was never picked on by the other kids over it.

Pause

So when did it all start? The bullying, you may ask. Well, the answer to that is when I got to senior school. I started senior school when I was aged 13 as a third former and was to be there for three years. It was three years of hell. And I bet you're thinking, yeah it'll be Liverpool fans who came from another junior school. No. It wasn't. The two kids I have mentioned were actually fellow United fans. I bet that's come as a shock. But it's true.

Pause

I had been apprehensive about starting senior school. I had heard all the rumours about been bullied and getting your head pushed down the toilet, that sort of thing. When I got there, some of the fourth formers were a bit rough. But to be honest, they didn't really bother me that much. I'd heard rumours there were two third year students making a name for themselves, which were the aforementioned. They apparently were taking over the house block. They were a lot bigger than all the other third year students and actually bigger and

14

rougher than the fourth year students. I heard they had given some of them a real beating. Kids from my junior school who were in the same house block as me warned me not to go into the block at break time as they would do something to me. They told me they had been particularly unpleasant to Liverpool fans, as they supported United. Unfortunately, I was led into a false sense of security. I thought fellow United fans and all that.

Pause

One day I decided to go into the house block. I had my United scarf and bag with me. All my books were in my bag. I casually walked into the house block and to my locker. As I was putting some of my books away I felt the presence of someone behind me. It was Baines. I turned round to meet him. We sort of looked at each other for what seemed like an age. I decided to break the ice. 'Good win on Saturday,' I said. 'Never thought Leicester could win at our place.' He didn't speak. Then he was joined by Collins. 'Well, what do we have here?' Collins muttered. 'Some silly pratt who doesn't know the rules of the house block,' said Baines. 'I think he needs to understand that he needs permission to come in here.' 'Permission,' Collins said. Like an echo. With that I was dragged bodily around the house block to the toilet. My head was rammed fully down the pan and it was flushed. I was choking as I had inhaled water. I was then punched and kicked at will. It was so traumatic that I nearly blacked out. When I was telling Donna about it I broke down and wept like it was happening to me now.

Pause

She had to pause the session and get me a glass of water. After about five minutes, she asked, 'Are you okay to carry on, David?' I agreed to. I then told her how it carried on from there. Whenever they saw me in the corridor, anywhere really, I was beaten. They locked me in a cupboard just before a lesson once. A cleaner let me out eventually. I received detention for that, because I had missed a lesson and was deemed to have played truant. I was too frightened to tell any of the teachers what I was going through in case of reprisals. If my mother saw any bruises on my body, I would just say I got them in PE. This is when I became very withdrawn. I was really depressed. At all my sessions with Donna we go through all of the incidents and she tells me to talk openly. She is always talking about closure and moving on. I know this is what I need to do. But it's easier said than done.

Fade

Scene Two

Lights up

David sits on a chair in the works canteen.

I don't want you to think that all the sessions I have with Donna are all crying and yelling, that sort of thing. Although I do vent my anger by punching a punch bag when I get really into the feeling. If United have won on the weekend we talk about that. Donna must watch the football results to see what mood I will be in. She always knows the score. I can imagine her sitting and taking notes when the results come in. She always seems to know a great deal about the match. The score, and who scored and man of the match. This is to balance out the session, so it's not all negative. If United have lost, she finds something else to talk about to ensure that the hour long session isn't all intense. The session that I have just had was one such session. United had just lost on the weekend, so we talked about other things. She asked me what my week had been like. I brought two events into the conversation and we spent the whole hour discussing them.

Pause

I spoke about both events quietly as I didn't really feel like getting too emotional. I spoke first about something to do with the generosity of a work colleague and saved the really big event until the second part of the session. I told Donna that when I had got to work on Monday I had an unexpected surprise in my locker. United are due to play Liverpool in a Champions League game at Old Trafford in a fortnight's time. Tickets are like gold dust. I managed to get my hands on one because I am a season pass holder and we got first refusal. Which is only fair. I wasn't the only one going to the game, Jim who I work with was also going. Apparently, he had bought two tickets, but couldn't go because there had been a sudden death in the family and the funeral was on the day of the match and on the other side of the country. He put them in an envelope with a short note and popped them in my locker. The note just explained the situation and he asked that either I use them or give them to someone who wants to go. I was flabbergasted. Donna was so pleased when I told her. 'See David, you can make friends. He obviously likes you.' She said. The dilemma was who I gave them to. I wasn't going to sell them on the black market, it just wouldn't be right.

Pause

Anyway, then we got to the big one. I had to take a deep breath over this one. I do a United blog. Just a few lines after a game. I give the team and the players marks out of ten. That sort of thing. I also ask for comments from other fans. Well, you could have blown me away. I only get a comment from Baines. He agreed with my comments and also informed me of a school reunion that he was organising and asked if I would like to go. Donna asked me how I felt about it. I replied that I was a bit apprehensive about meeting him again. This prompted over use of a therapist's favourite word – closure. Over the next thirty minutes, that word kept coming at me like I was stood at the bottom of a mountain and an avalanche suddenly erupted. 'If you meet him again and he is nice to you it will bring closure, David.' She kept saying. 'What if he isn't?' I said, 'and what if Collins is with him?' 'People change David, especially when they get older,' she respond-ed. 'I think they will want to make amends.' She then brought in the two football tickets. 'David, you could show real generosity and hold out the hand of friendship and give them these two tickets for the football match. That will speak volumes of you as a person. You will have forgiven,' she said.

Pause

Anyway, we left it that I would think about it over the weekend and then respond to him. I just don't know what to do. I have visions of turning up at some pub or other and seeing these two bullies and feeling really vulnerable again. But on the other hand, if I went I would be proving to them that I am not that little scared boy any-more. I am certainly bigger now, more muscular thanks to joining the local gym and hiring a personal trainer. Actually, I am warming to the idea. If I do go, I'll wear my tight fitting training top, the one that shows off my biceps. I hope they've let themselves go and are fat lumps with a great big beer belly. It wouldn't surprise me. They weren't renowned for attending the PE sessions at school, they generally twagged.

Pause

Yes, I think I will attend after all.

Gets up from the chair.

Fade

17

Scene 3

Lights up

David sits on a park bench. He is casually dressed with a Manchester United scarf around his neck.

Well it's the big day. Thousands of United fans attending tonight's game against the team we all love to hate – Liverpool. Apparently it's a sell-out, just short of 70,000. Liverpool got 15,000 tickets. They're all in the Scoreboard End; there has to be segregation of the fans because of a history of trouble. The atmosphere is going to be electric. I'm getting picked up by coach in the next half an hour. Anyone who is anyone will be there. Thousands of people have been disappointed. It really does pay to be a season pass holder. I got my ticket online. I didn't even have to queue. And to think some people couldn't get any tickets, I ended up with two spare.

Pause

So what did I do with those extra tickets I hear you ask. I did what Donna suggested. I gave them to Baines and Collins. I attended the school reunion. They were there, full of themselves they were. Some people never change. I got no apology for what they did to me. I guess in a way I didn't expect one. The bullying subject never came up in the conversation. But Baines made sure he came over to me from the start. We had a conversation about this and that, jobs, relationships etc, etc. Then we got onto United. He knew I was still active as he read my blog. He went when he could get a ticket. He'd been working away for a few years and was on the waiting list for a season pass. When he came back to the North West he looked up Collins and decided to organise a school reunion as well as go to watch United again. Collins wasn't a season pass holder either and he joined the waiting list too. We got onto the Liverpool game and that's when I said about the spare tickets. When I offered them for nothing the pair of them were ecstatic. They couldn't thank me enough. I had them on me and I handed them over. I spoke to a few more people and stayed until the end. A good night all round really.

Pause

The following day I had a session with Donna. She just beamed when I told her what I had done. 'Oh David that's just brilliant,' she said.

18

'What a gesture.' Then I got that word again: 'closure.' 'This will bring real closure on all those issues David. To forgive is divine,' she said, with a real satisfied look on her face. 'How did it make you feel?' she asked. 'Okay. I guess,' I muttered. 'Well I think it will take a bit of time to sink in. Big steps like this take some time before you realise the magnitude of your actions,' she said. We spent the rest of the session talking about how many more sessions I will need given that I had taken this giant step. She told me she had seen such a change in me from when we first started the sessions. She felt that talking about the bullying was powerful in itself, but forgiving was much more powerful. She finished the session by telling me that I should congratulate myself for showing such courage.

Pause

With all this going on I'm in danger of losing sight of the friendship shown to me. I almost forgot to thank the person who had shown me such friendship in the first place. The person who had given me the tickets so that I could pass them on. As I alluded to earlier, I don't always make friends easily. The scars of an unhappy childhood can come into adult life. It was really nice of Jim to think of me, especially in the circumstances, the family funeral and all that. I know he was looking forward to the game because he told me so in the staff canteen. He told me he was taking his younger brother who was really excited about going to the game, and had talked about nothing else since the draw was made.

Pause

Anyway, I got him two cards. One was a sympathy card, it had a nice message inside. The other was a thank you card for giving me the tickets. In the latter card I wrote a short note telling him what I had done with the tickets. I didn't want him to feel that I had made money out of his situation. I have today and tomorrow off. But I made sure that I went to work to leave my cards in his locker. I know he's in tomorrow as he just got the one day off to attend the funeral.

Pause

I went straight into the locker area. Jim's locker is easy to find. It's the bright red one. And it's got his nickname on it: 'Scouser'. Yes that's right. Jim's a Scouser. He's a Liverpool supporter. He would have been in the Scoreboard End with all the other Liverpool fans: 15,000 of them. But of course, now things have changed. It will have 14,998 Liverpool fans in there and two United fans.

Pause

(*Sighs.*) As I said, tickets were hard to come by. I'm sure the Liverpool fans will give Baines and Collins a real Scouser's welcome. Glad I brought my binoculars. I'm high up in the adjacent stand. (*Gets up from the bench.*) Ah, here's the coach now. Well, must dash.

Ends

Election

Andrew is 38 and lives alone. He works at a betting shop.

Setting:

Scene 1, 2 & 3: Chair

Performance time:

10 minutes

Scene 1

Andrew sits in a chair in the staff room of where he works.

It's always difficult to find a job when you have a chequered work history. I was two years between jobs, before I got this one. It was very difficult to move on from what was the worst period of my life. I was sacked from the job I loved because of something I was accused of doing – embezzlement. The worst thing someone in this profession can be accused of. I fought it tooth and nail because I was not guilty of the crime. Someone else was, and I knew who it was but couldn't prove it. I was sacked on the grounds of gross misconduct. It affected me greatly, losing my job. My self-esteem sunk, my partner left me and I was hit financially. I had to down size my property which meant me selling my lovely flat in the centre of town to buy a modest terraced house across town.

Pause

Everything was going great at work until a new manager came into the office by the name of John Riley. Riley came with a reputation. One of the girls said she had heard that he had left his last job 'under a cloud.' She reckoned that he had wandering hands where the female staff were concerned and that he had a gambling habit. I never took to the guy at all. He was very overweight, you could often smell alcohol on his breath and he was forever outside having a fag. Not very professional at all.

Pause

Things started to happen shortly after he started. It was about a week into his role when he got us all together and said he had had some money stolen from his wallet which he had left in the staff room. We all just looked at one another. Then Gill, the girl who had heard a little about him said, 'are you accusing someone here of stealing your money?' 'No,' he replied. 'I just want to know if anybody has seen anything. That's all.' We said we hadn't. We left the meeting with a real feeling of resentment. Gill said she felt he was trying to create a feeling of mistrust amongst us, and that he was more than likely going to be up to something, and if he could also claim to be a victim then people wouldn't suspect him. It made sense.

Pause

Then there started to be issues with him and Gill. She said he had joked about one or two personal things that she didn't feel comfortable with. I advised her to go to head office with a complaint. She was reluctant to do this. We noticed that money was going missing from the takings. Then out of the blue, my shifts were changed. I was told that until further notice I would be working a Sunday and I was also working a lot of evenings. I also noticed I was being kept away from working with Gill. We got on so well together. There was nothing going on between us, we were just good friends and work colleagues.

Pause

I hated the Sunday shift. It was unsociable and carried more responsibilities. I had to take responsibility for the whole takings for the weekend. Riley didn't work weekends, he was a nine to five Monday to Friday guy. But it was working the Sunday that gave me an insight into Riley and his gambling habit. It is standard practice at any betting shop that staff are not allowed to gamble in their own shop. Anyone who wants to place a bet generally went to one of our competitors or did it online. However, I discovered Riley's gambling was the slot machines, or one arm bandits as they are known in the trade. I would pass an amusement arcade on my way to work and on my way home and I would see him in there on a machine every Sunday. He'd be there in the morning and the evening. So it was obviously a serious habit he had.

Pause

Just when I thought things couldn't get any worse – they did. Gill left. Rather than put up with Riley's behaviour, she sought pastures new. Little did I know that our paths would cross again.

Fade

Scene 2

Lights up

Andrew sits in a chair in his lounge at home.

February the fourteenth, two years ago. A time etched in my memory forever. What should have been a great time was an absolute nightmare. Thanks to Riley. It was the day I was suspended and the day my girlfriend left me.

Pause

I got to work as normal at 8.30 a.m. prompt. It was a Friday. I came out of the staff room and headed for the office ready to start my shift. Riley appeared from nowhere and said, 'Andrew I need to see you now in my office.' I replied, 'what about?' 'You'll find out very shortly,' he said. I entered his office and there sitting behind his desk was a guy from head office, name of Taylor. I had spoken to him over the telephone on numerous occasions. I sat down when I was invited to. Riley started the conversation. He said, 'Andrew since you have worked the Sunday shift the weekend takings have been down. It's all documented.' Taylor said, 'how do you explain this?' 'I don't know,' I murmured. Riley put the documentation on the table and I was invited to inspect it. I put my glasses on and sure enough every weekend taking was down from the first date that I had commenced the weekend shift. I got flustered in there and couldn't even put a coherent sentence together. Taylor said, 'we have no alternative but to suspend you.' He then went through the disciplinary procedures.

Pause

Two weeks later I attended a disciplinary that was basically a 'kangaroo court.' I was sacked with immediate effect. Three years' hard work counted for nothing. I was broken. Kate, my partner left me on the day I was suspended, Valentine's Day. She wouldn't believe me when I told her that I had done nothing wrong and had been stitched up. I was left with nothing. And to make matters worse, the person who I knew had stitched me up, Riley, came up to me after the hearing, when I was shell shocked, put his hand on my shoulder and said, 'never mind Andrew, something else will turn up.' I never responded. I just couldn't. I couldn't say in the hearing that it was him, because I had no proof.

Pause

It was when I moved house that I bumped into Gill again. It's funny how things work really. She was living in the next street. Her marriage had broken up and she had moved out of the marital home and took her young son with her. She invited me in for coffee one day and we got talking. I told her what had happened. She wasn't at all surprised, and was certainly a lot more sympathetic than my ex had been. It turned out that Riley had been sexually harassing her, which is why she left. She didn't want all the hassle of complaining about him.

Pause

She was working for a rival bookmakers and said that she would put in a good word for me. And this is how I came to get a new job. The boss was a woman, Jo. She was very understanding and I think she knew about Riley. Anyway, she gave me a chance, a second opportunity and I've never looked back.

Pause

I was just getting over Riley when something happened that brought back all the old memories.

I was just sat in my house reading the morning paper when I heard the letterbox sound. I went to look to see what had come through. I was inquisitive as it was a little early for the postman. It turned out to be a leaflet from the Labour Party. I looked at it and there staring at me was a picture of Riley. He was introducing himself as the candidate in the forthcoming local elections. I contacted Gill straight away. Not only had she got one but she had found out that her son, Martin, had delivered it. Apparently, Riley had seen him sat on a bench and had asked him if he wanted to make some money. He offered him £10 to deliver three streets.

Pause

Gill saw me at work and informed me that she'd heard Riley had left his role as manager at the other bookmakers before he was sacked. He had been caught with his fingers in the till and had two cases of sexual harassment levied against him.

Pause

It was obvious he had duped the Labour Party into endorsing him as a candidate. He could charm the birds out of the trees, that one. We both decided then and there that he had to be stopped. And there was no time to lose.

Fade

25

Scene 3

Lights up

Andrew sits once again in a chair in his lounge.

The election was barely four weeks away. We knew that we didn't have a lot of time. We ruled out approaching the Labour Party and informing them of what we knew. It just wouldn't have worked. After all, he had not been sacked, and I had. He would have just discredited me if we had done that. It was during a 'what to do session' that I had a brilliant idea. Gill said, 'I will tell Martin that he can't leaflet for him anymore. I don't want my son helping that individual in any way.' 'No,' I said. 'He should continue.' 'What and work to get Riley elected?' she replied. 'No,' I said. 'We let Riley think that his leaflets are going out when in fact they are not.' I knew that our two streets and the other street that Martin was told to deliver to were extremely important streets. All three had about three hundred houses. That's nine hundred in all. If most had more than one adult living in them then we could be talking about nearly two thousand potential voters.

Pause

I made an offer there and then to Gill. I said, 'Tell Martin that I will pay him £10 not to deliver the leaflets. Well, not all of them anyway.' I can be really cunning when I want to be. I knew that some people would put up Labour posters in the window. They would more than likely be members of the party. If they didn't get a leaflet then they would know that something was wrong. So, I told Gill to tell Martin that when he gets the next batch and any further ones, he should only deliver to the ones with a Labour poster in the window. 'It's a win, win,' I said. 'Martin gets paid twice and only delivers a few leaflets instead of nine hundred. And we get to stop a cretin from getting into a position of power.'

Pause

Gill liked the idea, and so did Martin. All in all, Martin got six more leaflet drops to do. It took him a fraction of the time and he got £20 instead of £10. That's good business in anyone's books. It worked a treat. Riley kept giving him the rounds so he never suspected anything; and the Conservatives and the Liberal Democrats leafleted the full three streets.

Pause

Gill and I both decided that it wasn't enough for Riley to lose, we wanted to be there to see it. Gill had seen an advert in the local paper asking for people to count the votes in the Guildhall after the votes had been cast. We both applied and on the form we were sent we were asked if we had a preference to which ward we wanted to work on. We both indicated that we wanted the ward where we resided. And we were both successful.

Pause

The day of the election came and we were both at work. We didn't talk about it. We both felt it was best to stay silent, so as not risk being overheard. We left work at the same time and quietly went to the polling station and cast our votes. We then went back to my house, had a meal and looked forward to the evening. Nothing was certain. It might not have worked. But it certainly was not in Riley's favour to not be able to get his message out to the full electorate.

Pause

At 9.30 p.m. we set off to the Guildhall. We both felt very nervous. If he won anyway, he would have the last laugh. It was a gamble what we had done. But neither of us regretted anything.

Pause

Just after 10.00 p.m. all the votes started to come in, as did the candidates and their supporters. You should have seen Riley's face when he saw us. He was laughing and joking until he saw us both, then his face dropped. It was a picture.

Pause

All the boxes were emptied one by one and an initial check was done to verify that the number of votes cast tallied with the amount that the returning officer had said were cast. Then we got onto the vote itself. It was clear it was going to be close as the evening wore on with all three major parties neck and neck. We finished the counting and then an officer started to tot up the votes for each candidate. It seemed to take an age. He then got the candidates together and informed them that he was ready to call the result. He went alphabetically he said, 'Brown, Liberal Democrat: 2,209; Carter, Conservative: 2,330.' There was a loud cheer from those wearing blue rosettes. Then he said. Riley, Labour party, 2,339. The cheering was deafening. Gill and I looked at each other and our hearts sank. Then we looked at Riley who was been mobbed. He just grinned at us. Our plan had failed. But then we heard a little voice coming from a woman in the blue corner, 'Recount. We want a recount,' she said. Riley's face dropped. The cheering stopped. The woman pointed to Riley's batch of votes and said, 'we believe some of our votes are in there.'

Pause

Well talk about drama. We counted again and then again. We were all there until 5.00 a.m. It was unbelievable. The first recount the Conservatives won and Labour demanded another recount. When we did it again the Conservatives won again and because the vote tallied with the first recount the returning officer refused a further recount. Carter won for the Conservatives by the narrowest of margins, nine votes to be exact. Neither of us supported the Conservatives but we were elated. But we couldn't show our feelings. We had to be professional. But I just couldn't resist one final word with Riley. I walked up to him and I said, 'Never mind something else with turn up.'

Ends

Numbers

Carla is in her early 30s. She has just started a new job in a call centre. She is on a six month trial. She doesn't mind the work but dislikes one of her colleagues.

Setting:

Scene 1 & 2: Stool

Scene 3: Chair

Performance time:

10 minutes

Scene One

Carla sits alone in the staff canteen. She is dressed smartly.

Honestly, I really don't know who she thinks she is. Stuck up cow. I am referring to one of my colleagues, unfortunately. Well, I say colleague, if that's the best way of describing her. Lucy, they call her, works directly opposite me. Always running off to the supervisor telling tales. You know the sort. She's had it in for me from day one. Reporting me for been late back from lunch, not advising a client correctly, etc, etc. Someone said she's got money problems. Behind on her rent and got the council on her back for council tax arrears. Something to do with some ex who took all her money and then cleared off. Not my problem really. The job would be okay if it wasn't for her. Anyway, she's always looking at ways of making money. As soon as I started she pestered me to buy a raffle ticket at a £1.00 a go or £5 for a strip. I said, 'what's the prize?' She said, 'a microwave.' I said, 'I've got one, I don't need another thank you.' And I put my purse away. She really took the hump.

Pause

Then it was the lottery. She decided that the fifteen of us who work in the call centre section should form a syndicate and do the lottery. I agreed to this as it's only a quid each and I like the idea of playing, and you never know what can happen. People and syndicates have won millions. Anyway, Lucy starts to take over everything, made us all sign a contract to ensure that any winnings were fairly distributed, as long as everyone contributed. I saw no problem with that. But then she starts to dictate how we are going to play. And we had an enormous bust up over this. I didn't know what she was up to when she came over to me and asked me for my date of birth. I thought it was for office birthday cards and presents. I didn't realise she was going to use everyone's birthday and a few lucky numbers thrown in for good measure to calculate the lottery numbers. When I found out I said it was ridiculous to use that system. 'Well if you've got a better idea,' she said, 'let's hear it.' I said, 'number predictions. Certain numbers come out more regular than others and it's a case of calculating using the numbers drawn the previous weeks to predict what will occur next.' 'All sounds very complicated to me,' she said. 'And who's going to do all that messing around every week?' 'I will,' I said.

Pause

Anyway, we couldn't agree. One of the other girls suggested a compromise. Do it one way one week and the other the following week. I wasn't totally happy with this, but I reluctantly agreed. I thought it was best. Keep the peace and all that. Anyway, the first week we did her system and got one number. Which, as luck would have it, was my birthday the tenth. 'We're never going to win like this,' I said. 'You'll see,' she said.

Pause

Anyway, then it was my turn the following week. I worked on it over the weekend on my computer. I put the numbers that had just been drawn and looked back at previous numbers and calculated from that the likely six numbers. I sat at home when the results were given – but not one number was called. When I got to work on the Monday morning she was full of herself, she was. I could see her throughout the day talking to all the other girls on a one to one and then giggling like silly children. I think she actually enjoyed losing that week. It seems to me that she would much rather prove me wrong than actually win. I'm sure of it. Well, I think she wants to win, but in her week if you see what I mean. She wouldn't refuse the winnings if my system came up trumps. She'd have the money spent before she got her share.

Pause

Well I'm confident that my system will work. It just might take a while to come to fruition, that's the thing. And I don't know if I can stand working with her for much longer. But we'll see in the coming weeks and months whose system proves to be the winning one. We'll see.

Gets up from chair.

Fade

Scene 2

Lights up

Carla sits alone in the staff canteen once again.

Well, what a six months I've just endured. Thanks to Lucy I am now doing a new job and have missed out on a share of a lottery win. That woman is the absolute pits. She continued to make life as difficult as possible for me at every opportunity, complaining every time I made a mistake. The company decided to give me another chance when my six month probation came to an end. They suggested that I move into another section, the finance department so that I am not in direct contact with Lucy any more. They have started me on another six month probation, but I'm fine with that. I know that I am good at my job. I could do the other job if it hadn't been for super bitch. Anyway, finance is more my thing.

Pause

I'm happy here, the people are nice. It seems that Lucy is well known for her unpleasantness. They all know about her in the office. She has a bit of a reputation. I'm glad I'm away from her but I hate that she has had the last laugh. When I left the office, apparently I duly left the syndicate. This is according to Lucy's rules, of course. I challenged it but lost; and I challenged it because the week after I left the office they won. Using the birthday and lucky number system. And if that wasn't bad enough, the person who took my place in the office and subsequently joined the syndicate, had a birthday the tenth of the month the same as me. Different month but that was irrelevant. They won using the same numbers as they would have done had I been there, and it was the line with the 10 in it that came through. That's what hurts the most. They won £30,000 for five numbers. When I knew I was leaving I informed one of the other girls that I wanted to remain in the syndicate and offered my £1.00. Lucy got to know about it and took great pleasure in informing me that once you leave the office you leave the syndicate. I said that I still worked for the organisation, but she was unrepentant. When they won and I complained and asked for my share she sent me an email clarifying that I was no longer in the syndicate given that I had moved office, it was call centre staff only. She also advised in the email that I should start up a syndicate in my new office.

Pause

Just to rub things in, she makes sure that she walks past the finance office at every opportunity with a stupid smirk on her face, and wearing some new outfit. She could never afford new clothes before because of her debts, but she can now. Anyway, I asked the girls in the finance office if they wanted to form a syndicate and they all agreed. There's only ten of us in here. I told them about my system and being finance people they understood more. 'Sounds good,' said Karen who sits at the next desk.

Pause

We've only just started and we've been doing the Wednesday lottery tickets as well as the Saturday one. Just to give us a bit more of a chance. I've been put in charge of the numbers which I really don't mind at all. I calculate everything and purchase the tickets twice a week. Nobody complains. I've explained that this could be the long game. At present playing this system twice a week for a fortnight hasn't generated anything yet, but I'm hopeful. I feel the pressure a bit given what happened with the call centre lot, but I am not going to be swayed by what was really a stroke of luck. However, life moves on.

Pause

I would just like to wipe that smug grin off her face. I just hope they don't win again or I could face real pressure from my new colleagues to change the system. I got the idea from watching the film *The Imitation Game*, about the mathematician Alan Turing. I'm sure if he had had a choice of systems to use to crack the Enigma code he would have chosen my system over the birthday and lucky number system. Don't think the Ministry of Defence would have been too impressed if he'd used the latter, somehow!

Gets up from the chair and walks towards the door.

Fade

Scene Three

Lights up

Carla sits alone in the lounge of her house. She is casually dressed.

It's three months since I spoke to you last, and what a three months it has been. I've had to employ the services of a solicitor; and they don't come cheap, I can tell you. So what has been the issue? I hear you say. (*A beaming smile*). Well, my system came through I'm happy to say. But it was not without its problems. Just after I spoke to you last, all six number came up. We won £6,000,000. We were all ecstatic. The champagne was flowing at my house I can tell you. As soon as those numbers were drawn out everyone descended on my place. It was bedlam. I've never been so popular.

Pause

We all decided to carry on as if nothing had happened. We went to work as normal and just got on with our jobs. Lucy carried on being a super bitch as usual. Appearing in the office at every opportunity to show off something new she had purchased, clothes or jewellery usually. Nobody at work suspected a thing, but then the papers got hold of it and everything went sky wards. We did a photo shoot opening a bottle of champagne and gave interviews. The usual thing you would expect. We were asked what we going to spend the money on. We all said the same thing that we hadn't really thought about it. Quite frankly, I could have done without all the fuss. It just attracts attention.

Pause

And attract attention it did. One of the girls had let it be known to the press that I was the 'genius' behind the win, because I used a system based on prediction. Talk about setting the hare racing. Lucy picked up on that straight away. She came bursting into the office with some of the call centre staff. She came right up to me and said, 'it's all one syndicate. You used the system that you used with us and we would have won had you stayed in the department. But because you chose to transfer you negated your side of the contract.' I said, 'I was offered a transfer and took it because of your behaviour and I didn't get a cut from your winnings.' Basically, I sent her away with a flea in her ear. 'We'll see about that,' she yelled as she was going out of the door. The next thing I knew I got a solicitor's letter informing me that unless the call centre staff were included in the winnings that I would be taken to court.

Pause

I was worried sick about it. I've never had to deal with a solicitor before, well not for anything like this. When I was buying my house, yes. But not to seek advice on something like this. Anyway, I saw a solicitor with the rest of the syndicate. We were advised not to spend any of the money until the matter was resolved and told not to speak to anybody about it. This was a bit difficult as we all worked for the same company. Our solicitor wrote to the call centre's solicitor and informed them that we were not going to include them in the winnings and that if they should want to take the matter further then they should take the matter to court.

Pause

We then received notification that this is what they were doing. The morale of the office dipped severely when we got notified of this. The rest of the office nominated me to be the spokesperson. A role I wanted all along. The call centre staff nominated Lucy. It was 'pistols at dawn' as far as I was concerned. The office might have been quiet but at least we didn't have to put up with Lucy appearing throughout the day. She must have been advised to stay away.

Pause

We got to a date being set for a hearing. My solicitor informed me we were at a stage of exchanging documents. He had requested theirs. It was just a copy of the syndicate contract that I had signed. One of the clauses said that a member must stay working for the company. Tick. And must have paid for that particular week. Not tick. My solicitor asked if I had anything to counter this. I said, 'it's funny you should say that, I was looking through my past emails and came across this one from Lucy after they had won £30,000.' I got the paper version out of my bag and gave it to him. There was a long pause and he said, 'Well your former colleague appears to have "shot herself in the foot", she's informed you in writing that as you no longer work in the department that the syndicate was set up in and you had not paid the subscription you were exempt from claiming any winnings. She can't have one rule for her department and another for yours. I must fax this across at once.'

Pause

Later that day he contacted me and said that they had pulled the case. He also said that because they had initiated the action they have to pay the legal costs. He said, 'I wish you could have shown me the document sooner, so that we could have prevented the plaintiff having to pay costs.' I said, 'I just forgot about the email. I've had so much on my mind.'

Pause

As my mother use to say: 'Slowly, slowly catchy monkey.'

Ends

Picture

Jennifer is in her early 30s. She is very attractive. She works as an IT consultant. She advises companies on Internet security. She has just split from her long term boyfriend and has decided to try Internet dating. She feels very awkward about it but feels it is worth a try. All her friends are in serious relationships and she does not want to go out alone searching for love.

Setting:

Scene 1 & 2: Chair

Scene 3: Stool

Performance time:

10 minutes

Scene 1

Jennifer sits in a chair in her lounge. She is casually dressed.

It was Mia, one of my colleagues, who recommended online dating. 'Everyone's doing it,' she said. She made it sound so appealing. She said I will get loads of dates. She recommended a site and during our lunch break she took photographs of me, uploaded them and created my profile. She said, 'you'll get loads of replies, but only go on dates with guys that you fancy and watch out for the weirdoes.' Wise words. But how are you supposed to spot them? I mean, do they state on their profiles that they're a weirdo?

Pause

Anyway, I started to get loads of responses, just as Mia said I would. I replied to all of them as I find it impolite not to. I stressed that I want someone who is reasonably successful. I earn a reasonable income, I don't necessarily want to meet a professional guy, but I don't want someone who empties my bins if you see what I mean. I like a man to look smart, not necessarily in a suit. Smart but casual. I know I'm a bit choosy but having standards is good. My mother always used to say to me when I was growing up, 'don't settle for second best.' And I won't.

Pause

Most of the guys who got in touch didn't tick all the boxes. Some didn't tick any at all. I went for a few coffee dates with some guys who made contact. But it was clear they were not for me. They didn't look much like their photographs in most cases. I think they might have been doctored. Some exaggerated their jobs. They made out they were practically running a department when they were actually the general 'dog's body.' I caught one guy out well and truly. We met for lunch and got on reasonably well. He asked me what I did and I told him that I worked in IT advising companies on Internet security. He told me he worked for a particular company as their Head of IT. 'So we have something in common,' he said with a great big smile on his face. I didn't tell him that after lunch I was booked to go to his company to work with their IT. I had been liaising with their Head of IT but it certainly wasn't him as the person was female.

Pause

Anyway, I thanked him for lunch. He asked to meet again and I suggested he contact me via the app. It wasn't a no, nor a yes. But more likely to be a no. I just don't like telling someone face to face that it's a no.

Pause

I went back to my office, got all my things together and set off to my next job, to meet the Head of IT at my lunch date's company. I entered the company's building and took the lift to the second floor. The doors opened and I was faced with the reception desk. And who is sat at the reception answering calls? My lunch date. He was a receptionist. His face was a picture. He was on the phone to a client when he saw it was me. The poor thing then had to call the Head of IT to let her know I was here. He never got back to me for a second date. Can't think why.

Pause

I carried on having lunch dates with guys that ended with a first date. I was giving up hope of meeting someone. Until I was contacted by Dan. He ticked all the boxes. It seemed the effort had paid off. I could put all the disappointments behind me.

Fade

Scene 2

Jennifer sits in a chair in her lounge. She is dressed to impress. There is a single glass of wine on the coffee table.

Mia warned me about weirdoes but she didn't go into great detail. I wish she had because I've just met one. And yes I'm referring to Dan. The man who ticked all the boxes. Only he ticked another box not on my list – pervert.

Pause

I did everything Mia said I should. She said, 'always meet them for lunch in a popular location. That way you are not at risk if he is strange, as you can get up and walk out.' So like all the others, I met Dan in a pub near where I work. I had seen his photograph and I liked what I saw. In his profile he had said he owned his own business installing security alarms. I checked this out by Googling his details and yes he did. Everything seemed too good to be true. And that's because it was.

Pause

The lunch date was a success. He arrived in his work clothes, which was fine. It was a working day and we had both come from our places of work. Nothing wrong with that. I didn't expect him to be in a suit and tie. He was in jeans and t-shirt. He looked good. He also had charm. The hour went very quickly I have to say. Some of the other lunch hour dates seemed a lot longer. We could have talked for hours. We may not have had the same line of work but we had the same musical tastes, liked the same films and we both had the same breed of dog. It seemed like an ideal match.

Pause

Mia said I should not break with routine. She advised that the guy should make the first contact if he wanted a second date. So when he asked to meet again I said he should contact me via the app. Which is what I said to all the other dates. Mia said, 'never let them know that you are too keen to meet again. Keep them guessing.' He just knew how to treat a woman. Or so I thought. He insisted on helping me on with my jacket. When we parted I was really nervous. I kept thinking, I hope I have not put him off contacting me again by stating that he should contact via the app. But Mia is the expert on these things. I am guided by her. When I got back to work I spoke to her. I told her everything and let on that I was really keen. I described him in great detail and said, 'I think I'm keen as well.' She told me that the protocol for the guy is to wait a couple of days before making contact. And that's exactly what he did. Something in the back of my mind was telling me this guy was a bit like Mia. He seemed to be well versed in this online dating thing. He told me he had only just joined and like me had just broken up with somebody and was looking for someone special.

Pause

He got in touch via the app as I had asked. I got a message telling me that he had enjoyed my company so much and that he would like to see me again. I replied that I had also enjoyed my meal in his company and would like to see him again. Messages went back and forth and we arranged to meet again at a different location. He chose the venue. It was a restaurant out in the country. I checked it out on the Internet and it seemed great. I love a nice meal out and I also like to be out of the city. The date seemed perfect. When I told Mia she was really jealous. She'd met this guy through online dating but she was getting a bit bored with him. I thought, well you are not getting your hands on mine lady.

Pause

The night of the second date came and I was so excited. I even bought a new outfit. I rushed home from work and went straight in the shower. I was sat in my bedroom putting my makeup on when my phone pinged. I thought, I hope he is not cancelling when I have gone to all this trouble. I hesitantly picked up my phone and when I saw it was from him my heart skipped a beat. I read the message it was short and it had an attachment. The message read: 'This is what's on the menu tonight.' Oh, I was so relieved. He was letting me see the menu before we arrived. I thought, well this is a real gentleman. I'll finish getting ready, then I'll have a quick browse of the menu.

Pause

So there I was all glammed up, makeup on, new outfit. Just about to go out of the door and I opened the message again and clicked on the attachment. It slowly opened to reveal (*Pause.*) a picture of Dan stood completely naked except for a tool holster belt. And he had a certain piece of his anatomy in his hand.

41

Pause

I just stood there completely aghast. Then my phone pinged again. It was another message from Dan, it read: 'so what do you think of the menu? Anything wet your appetite?' I just broke down. It was devastating. I didn't even bother replying. The whole night was ruined. Needless to say, I didn't go on the date.

Pause

When you write your profile on these sites. You don't put everything. Mia advised that you should always keep something back. Well in my case, I certainly did. I have a motto that I live by: Don't get mad, get even.

Gets up and walks to the door.

Fade

Scene 3

Lights up

Jennifer sits on a wooden chair in the kitchen of her friend Mia.

I'm just sat in Mia's kitchen whilst she telephones her boyfriend to tell him that he is now her ex with immediate effect. Then we are going out to celebrate what has been a most successful night. I told you about 'Dan the Man' as Mia likes to call him, and his antics. Well, Mia was not too impressed when I told her how the evening had unfolded.

Pause

Mia had rushed over to me at break time and asked how the date had gone. I explained what he did. 'Oh dear, you got a dick pic,' she said. She said that she had not warned me that, that could happen, as she didn't want to burst my bubble. I showed her the offending article. She laughed and then said, 'whatever you do, don't delete it.' Then she went off back to work. I got a message from her later asking me to come over to her place after work.

Pause

I knew she would be up to something. Mia is very bright. Maybe you should know a little bit more about her before I tell you want she did. Mia is our IT expert. When I go to companies I go to sell our Internet protection packages. I do a PowerPoint presentation. I tell them what we do, which basically is we stop people hacking into their computer system. Mia is the one who then goes to the company and installs the security system. She's an expert in her field. She's a poacher turned gamekeeper. She used to be a hacker herself. As daft as it seems, her criminal record got her the job in the first place.

Pause

All the time I was at work I was thinking about what we could do. Then I remembered I had accessed his work web page. He must have paid someone to create a web page for him to advertise his business. In my lunch hour I got his page up on my computer again. It was a very elaborate web page with him showcasing everything he does. At the top of the page the viewer is asked to click on letters of the alphabet. Each one had something behind it relevant to his work. A for alarm, C for contract, L for licence and W for warranty and so on. When you clicked on a letter an image would appear such as in the case of licence, a licence document stating that he is licensed to install alarms. It was all very cleverly put to together.

Pause

So I arrived at her flat about an hour ago. We had a brief chat and she uploaded the photograph onto her computer. I gave her the web address for his security company. She then got the page up. What she did next I can't even say, but she managed to get into the programme script. This is the script that tells the page what to say in the way of text and what to show. She somehow managed to get past the software security which was supposed to stop hackers. But then this comes as second nature to someone like her.

Pause

Then she told me to go and make some coffee and fix something to eat. She likes to work alone does Mia. She's a real Geek. Not quite a team player, if you see what I mean. Anyway, I duly obliged. After about half an hour she came through and we sat and had a snack. She said, 'I've finished by the way.' And she beckoned me to come through to the study to see his amended web page. She got the web page up and I looked at it and said, 'but it doesn't look any different to me.' 'Click on the letter W,' she said. I did and two images came up. The first one was the warranty that he gives with every alarm he installs and the second image is a photograph that informs people of what he is.

Ends

Whistler

Frances is in her early 50s and is a teaching assistant at a local primary school. She has been in post about 4 months after moving to the area. She lives in a quiet village where the school is located. She is divorced and lives alone.

Setting:

Scene 1, 2 & 3: Chair

Performance time:

10 minutes

Scene One

Frances sits in the staff room of the school. She is smartly dressed.

People often say they are in their dream job. I think it's a very over used phrase really. And the ones who say it are generally the ones who are earning mega bucks. Well, I can say it and I'm not earning mega bucks. I just love working with the children. They make the job, they really do. It's a good age four to eleven. They are so keen to learn. Then just when their hormones start to kick in, we pass them onto the senior schools. Couldn't be better really.

Pause

And the staff here are absolutely fantastic. I can honestly say that I have not had a single staff related problem since I've been here. The Head is so supportive and the teacher that I work with, Miss Jones, is the nicest person I think I have ever met. I have to refer to her as Miss Jones in a formal setting, it's Victoria in the staff room. Don't get me wrong, they're no pushovers. You are expected to do your job. Work hard. Put the children first. Well, I've no problem with that. I've always worked hard. I've built a reputation over the years for hard work. Never been out of work, not for a single day. When I've wanted to leave an organisation, I've never had a problem getting a reference from my employer.

Pause

I had to leave my last job very quickly. Don't worry, I hadn't done anything wrong. Far from it. I had a good job in London but I was going through a very messy divorce. I married a guy I met on the Internet. This was two years ago. I was reaching that age when a woman starts to think about things. I was approaching fifty and never been married. My mother kept telling me: 'Frances, if you don't meet someone soon, you'll be left on the shelf.' I guess I panicked and married the first available guy I met. I was very naive. Len's his name. He got in touch with me, said he liked my picture and profile. I met him a few times and the next thing he proposed. He actually went down on one knee when we were in a restaurant. People were applauding and the manager insisted we had a free bottle of champagne. It was all very romantic. The next thing I knew, we were in a church taking our vows.

Pause

I had a bit of money set aside just in case I did meet someone. Father had died when I had just turned twenty-one. He left me some money in his will. I'm an only child so I got the bulk of it. Mother was content with keeping the house they shared. He was well insured so their mortgage was paid off. Both he and mother always said that I should get on the property ladder as soon as possible. So I did. I bought a modest little house in the borough where I worked. I wasn't working as a teaching assistant then, I was working in a bank. I had a good income.

Pause

Anyway, I thought I'd won the lottery when I met Len. He was just a bit older than me and had a good job in the City, or so he told me. He moved into my house as soon as we were married. Everything was going well until I was contacted by a police woman out of the blue. She knocked on the door and asked for Len by name. I was working from home. Len was at work. She said that she needed to speak to him immediately. I rang him on his mobile. He answered and I told him that a PC Young wanted to speak to him. He just hung up. I never saw him again. I found out he was on the run from the police for stalking his previous partner, despite having a restraining order put on him. And the job in the City was a lie. He was employed by some dodgy character as a 'runner.'

Pause

When I spoke to the police officer I learnt he had met his last girl-friend on the Internet. And when she wanted out of the relationship, he hounded her day and night. I decided to leave my job and move. I had been attending night school to gain my qualifications as a teaching assistant because I was thinking of changing career sometime in the future. But events rather overtook me. I knew that I would have to leave the area. So when I saw this job advertised I applied and was successful. I sold the house and moved very quickly. Got a nice little cottage in a quiet village.

Pause

Everything was just falling into place when things started to happen.

Fade

Scene 2

Lights Up

Frances sits in a chair in her lounge. She is in her dressing gown.

As you can see from my attire I've only just got up. I've barely had a wink of sleep. The phone was ringing constantly throughout the night. When I got up to answer it, the line went dead. This has been going on for the last three nights. I thought it was my mother ringing me or the care home she is in. But no. I thought it is either a nuisance call or there is a fault. I called BT and they have confirmed that there is nothing wrong with the line. Given Len's previous behaviour I thought, to be on the safe side, I had better inform the police.

Pause

I also informed the Head Teacher of the situation. 'You must take the day off to recover,' she said. 'If you haven't had a good night's sleep, you won't be able to do your job properly.' She was very understanding. Then Victoria rang me to offer help and support. She's coming round on the weekend to see me. They've all been great. Except the police that is. Wonder when they'll get round here. Might not come at all. Priorities and all that.

Pause

I rang the local police station and they said they were busy at the moment but they might be able to send someone over later on in the evening. How very reassuring, I must say. I have been very guarded with who has my number. Obviously, I am ex-directory. I explained to the school my predicament and they were very understanding. I've been wracking my brain as to who else I have given my number to. I have joined one or two social gatherings. Well, you have to when you live on your own, otherwise you can get very lonely. I joined the village women's group. We meet a couple of times a month in the village hall and organise events aimed at involving other women in the village doing things. I don't know where I would be without the women's group. I really don't. They know about my predicament and have been very supportive. And the events have been great for me. Getting me out of the house for a start.

Pause

I discovered my love of baking again. When I was a child, I loved to bake with my mother. I just didn't have the time to bake when I got married and lived in London. Now, I've got time and have rediscovered my love for it. It was me who suggested we have a baking completion one weekend. Everyone was in agreement. It turned out that in the next village lived a former winner of *The Great British Bake Off*. It was decided to approach her to be the judge.

Pause

Well, you could have knocked me down with a feather when I won the competition. Val her name is, who was judging, she tasted everyone's cake. And then at the end she announced me as the winner. I got a rosette, a certificate and a box of chocolates. I was ecstatic. Everyone from the women's group were so pleased for me. Joan from next door was especially pleased for me. 'After what you've been through,' she said, 'richly deserved.' I often spend time at her house of an evening, and it has been known for a few glasses of wine to be sipped. She lives with her husband, Frank, and their teenage son, Paul. When I go across, Frank and Paul disappear and let us girls have some girlie time. We talk about things that women like to talk about. The men we've shared our lives with. I talk about Len and all the problems I had with him. His secretiveness mainly. She has a moan about Frank being a bit lazy at times and unromantic. I said, 'join the club on the latter. Half the women in the world complain about that one.'

Pause

After the first night of the nuisance calls, I went to see Joan and told her about it. She was very understanding. Joan was great to talk to. She said it sounded like my ex. We talked about that and the baking competition. From one extreme to another. We even joked about the fact that she was an avid baker and I a novice; but I came from nowhere and finished first and she finished fourth. I felt a lot better when I left her house. I really did.

Gets up from her chair.

Ah, here are the police now. Well, must dash.

Fade

Scene 3

Lights up

Frances sits in her lounge she is smartly dressed.

Well, it's certainly been a very interesting last two weeks, I can tell you. I can hardly catch my breath with all the goings on.

Pause

When the police finally arrived the other evening, I had a good chat with the young PC who came. I told him that the calls were every night and into the morning. He asked the inevitable question: 'Who do you think is responsible?' 'My ex,' I said. We then got into a long discussion about Len and his previous behaviour with his ex prior to meeting me. 'So he's got form,' he said. 'Yes,' I replied. He took notes and informed me that he would be looking into this as a top priority, vulnerable female and all that. He said that it might also involve CID.

Pause

The next thing I knew I had two plain clothes police officers knocking on my door, a man and a woman. We all had a good long chat. They asked if I was able to trace the call by doing the last caller number. I explained that I had done that and it came up as number not available. They explained that they had a very sophisticated piece of equipment which might be able to determine where the call was coming from. They asked me to keep a diary of when the calls occurred so they could map when was the best time to come and set the trap.

Pause

So over the next week or so I did just that. I recorded what time the calls came through and the duration. It drove me mad. I had to take time off work because of sleep deprivation. The school was very understanding. My doctor was fantastic as well. Basically, the calls were coming thick and fast throughout the late evening until the early hours.

Pause

I'm happy to say that someone has been arrested and will appear in court very soon on a charge of harassment. I bet you're thinking the police f tted the tracking device and caught the culprit red handed. Wrong. It was me. I caught them.

Pause

I was so unwell with it all, even with anti-depressants that the doctor prescribed. It was all getting to me. It was so difficult. The police advised not answering the call. So I left it. I rang my mother each night on my mobile to ensure that she was okay.

Pause

Anyway, the other evening I was sick with it and I just couldn't take anymore. I had had no sleep and was going down the stairs to make myself a drink at about 4 a.m., when the phone rang as I was walking past it. Without thinking I went against the advice of the police. I picked t up with one hand and with the other grabbed my school whistle that I keep hung up in the hall way. And I blew the whistle as hard as I could down the phone. I heard a noise of someone moaning at the other end.

Pause

It didn't ring again after that, and I actually was able to get to bed and sleep. I decided I would inform the police on waking what I had done. I rang f rst thing and spoke to the woman CID officer. She was very understanding and told me that she would come round later in the day. I felt quite chuffed with myself. I thought, I hope it's taught him a lesson.

Pause

I was so elated about it that I ran next door to tell Joan. I knocked on her door very excitedly. There was a long delay before the door opened. It was Paul, her son. I said, 'Is your mother in?' 'No,' he said. 'Father has taken her to hospital. She's got a perforated ear drum.'

Ends

www.ingramcontent.com/pod-product-compliance
Lightning Source LLC
Chambersburg PA
CBHW070609180626
46817CB00005B/2063